THERE'S A HIPPO
IN MY BATH!

Adapted from a story by Kyoko Matsuoka
Illustrated by Akiko Hayashi

DOUBLEDAY
NEW YORK   LONDON   TORONTO   SYDNEY   AUCKLAND

"It's bath time!" called my mother. Duckie and I were all ready. The bathroom door went rattle-rattle.

The floor was slippery,
so we had to be careful.

Duckie got in first.
"How's the water?" I
asked him. "Not too hot
and not too cold. Just
about right," he said.

So I jumped in too.
"How's the water?"
called my mother
from the kitchen.
"Not too hot and not too
cold. Just about right,"
I said.

I made my washcloth soapy and washed all over.

But Duckie didn't wash, he just played in the tub.

Bloop. Bloop. Bloop.

He dove down to the bottom.

But he quickly came up again.

"There's something down there," he said.

Blippety blop.

A great big turtle plopped out of the water.

"It's too hot up here on top of the ocean. On the
bottom it's nice and cool," said the turtle.

"But this isn't the ocean!" said Duckie.

"This is my bathtub," I said.

"Well then, what are those penguins doing
here?" asked the turtle.

I turned around and there were two penguins
standing behind me. They looked exactly alike.
I was so surprised I dropped my soap.
It slid all the way across the room.

Swoosh!

The two penguins took off, chasing

the soap. They slid on their tummies

over to a large, smooth rock.

But slowly the rock moved.

It opened its mouth and ate the soap.

It wasn't a rock at all.
It was a huge furry seal.
It began to blow bubbles
out of its mouth.

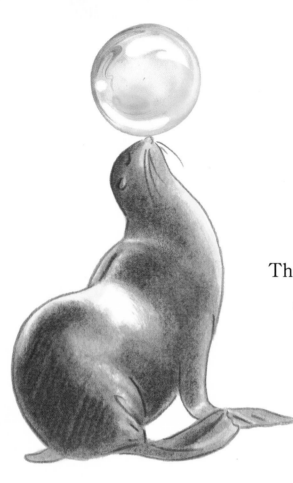

Then the seal began to blow
one big bubble.
It grew bigger
and bigger
and bigger
until . . .
Boom!
It popped.

"Oh dear,"

said a tiny voice behind me.

"That scared me!"

I turned around and there was

a great big fat hippopotamus.

"Would you mind giving my back a scrub?" it asked. "I can't quite reach it."

I scrubbed and rubbed the hippo
until it was soapy all over.
"Don't forget to wash behind my
ears," it said. "And between
my toes too."

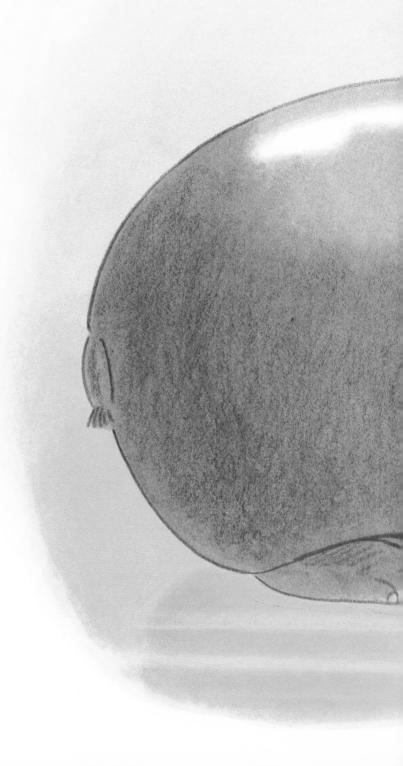

I washed behind the hippo's ears
and in between its toes.
I wondered how to rinse
the soap off when . . .

a shower of warm water
came from nowhere and washed
the suds away.
Behind me, in my tub
was a great big huge gigantic
whale, blowing its spout.

"All right, everybody," I said. "Let's go play in the tub."

Duckie splish-splashed in.

I jumped in.

The two penguins dove in.

The huge furry seal slid in.

The great big fat hippo made a
loud splosh.

And the great big huge gigantic
whale began to smile.

Then the two penguins started singing.

And the hippo joined in.

The turtle sang along

and so did Duckie.

When the whale opened its mouth to
sing I could see all the way down
to its stomach.
But then suddenly
I heard the bathroom door
go rattle-rattle.

My mother was coming in!

"What's all this rumpus about?" she asked.

But when I turned around,

everybody except Duckie had gone

under the water to hide.

"Well, did you and Duckie have a nice bath?" asked my mother.

"Oh yes," I said, "the best!"

Published by Doubleday, a division of
Bantam Doubleday Dell Publishing Group, Inc.
666 Fifth Avenue, New York, New York 10103

Doubleday and the portrayal of an anchor with a dolphin
are trademarks of Doubleday, a division of
Bantam Doubleday Dell Publishing Group, Inc.

Library of Congress Cataloging-in-Publication Data
Matsuoka, Kyoko, 1935–
There's a hippo in my bath!
Summary: A turtle, two penguins, a hippo, and a host
of other unlikely animals join a young boy in his bath.
[1. Baths—Fiction.   2. Animals—Fiction]   I. Hayashi,
Akiko, 1945–   ill.   II. Title.
PZ7.M43156Th   1989   [E]   88-28547

ISBN 0-385-26188-8
ISBN 0-385-26189-6 (lib. bdg.)

Text copyright © 1982 by Kyoko Matsuoka
Illustrations copyright © 1982 by Akiko Hayashi
Adaptation copyright © 1989 by Doubleday, a division of
Bantam Doubleday Dell Publishing Group, Inc.
Originally published by Fukuinkan Shoten, Tokyo 1982